ISBN: 9781980594406 Edition 2.1

CONTENTS

Acknowledgements

Bulimia
Epidemic
The Evil of the Yo-Yo
iCandy 2.0
The Moths Cometh Prelude
Orchard of Cacophony
Awoken
Flush
Paradox
Zombie
Squirm
Candle
Cemetery
I Miss U
Younger Than Laughter
The Moths Cometh
The Change Ring
Normal People
Scream
Morning
Gosling-bumps
The Halloween Poisoner
Happy X-mas
A Good Day 4 A Picnic
The Garden
Alice
Epithany Weird
Vibracia
Lost in the Mind of a Maniac, You're an Average Guy and Your Name is Jack
Scral-wal
Zidricdrake
Monster
Ghost in the Post

Not Even the Mad
Voice
Sweet Tusk
Childless
Abstract Poetry
Fragments
White Shed
A Finger to Your Lips
42
Sister Maria Luisa
Sad Farewell
Broken Doll
My Lil Poni Fucker
Waiting
It Lives Beneath London
Alone
Petrified
Discarded
The Uninvited (or Something Blue)
The Train is Late and Cremated
Umbrellas Up Unfurled
The House
Witchcraft
The Box of Be Careful What You Wish For
Florence and the Machine
Queen Mab's Revenge
The Raping Woods
Possessed
Mermaids & Pirates
Ghost of Wasp
Night Night
Your Turn
Queen of the Night
Unforgettable
Creepy Pasta
The Day the Aliens Didn't Come to Earth

Acknowledgements

To my beloved and wonderful
Ashleigh,
for amongst, many many other things,
thinking up the sub-title of this book

and to the various other people, animals*,
deities and spirits, who have also inspired me throughout the past twenty years, during which, poems appearing in this compilation were written.

Thank you for being you.

*people are animals, and animals are people

BULIMIA!

The most beautiful thing
Is thee change ring
The power to be who you are
Suspenders and stockings and bra
A chainsaw orgasm
In a broken down car
The power to play
Every inch of the day
And go just that little bit far

Straight to extreme
Where the air makes you scream
As it pushes your heart
Through your lungs
And every sweet kiss
So tender so bliss
Demands the delinquence of tongues

Do you know who I am
Said the corpse in the pram
As with your pale fingers
You push out its eyes
And then there is pain
As your drool drips like rain
As from its limp body she cries

With a shudder of joy
You destroy your best toy
Smash out its mind on the wall
And then there is gore
That drips from the whore
Forming an eloquent pool

The birds of ill omen
Sip at their cider
Closing their legs
Then opening wider

And the chainsaw melody stops
As the knife from your fingers just drops!

Epidemic

When deadly, diseases
Fly by sneezes
And people
Fly by plane

It only takes
A week or two
Then
Very few
Remain

It's hard to be
Terrified
At every little cough

It's hard to see
Your loved ones die
As bits of them, fall off!

It's hard to find
You're all alone
Last human
In your city
But joy returns
Quick to your heart
When greeted by
A kitty!

The Evil of the Yo-Yo!!

Children, slaves on strings
The Yo-Yo is their master
Tells them when to move
And then it tells them faster!

iCandy 2.0

It may be
Twenty Forty Four
When the woman you adore
Is assembled by machine
On a polished factory floor

She's exactly what you wanted
What you asked the website for
She reminds you of that girl
You knew
And fucks you like a whore

But there's always more:

Candy's an accomplished cook
Perfection on a plate
But your dinner
Starts to taste
Peculiar
On the days that you are late

She doesn't like Wendy
A little jealousy is cute
But you have to think
It's gone too far
When Wendy's found
In Candy's car
Unconscious and tightly bound
Amidst the shopping
In the boot

Of course
You ignore the problem
Because the sex is great
And the literature assures you
She's not capable of hate

But one evening
When upon you
In a state of pure gyrate
She puts her hands
About your neck
And seals your sorry fate!

The Moths Cometh Prelude

The Moths Cometh
So be you taught
Of little things
With little thought
For anything
Except their own
Within your corpse
They'll make their home.

Orchard of Cacophony

In the Orchard of Cacophony
Beneath an apple tree
Sat amidst the bluebells
The creature Poetry

Her eyes are supernovas
Orbiting blackholes
And her pretty nails are painted
With the blood of tortured souls

There in her hand
Gently held, a lady bug
She smiles as she squishes it
And signs it, with love.

AWOKEN

Early bird
Develops a headache
And goes back to bed
By mid afternoon
Besides
Night owls don't eat worms!

FLUSH

She enters the room to unfamiliar faces
Walls covered in pictures in places
She pulls up her skirts
And sits schizophrenically down
Lace around her ankles
Room with a loo!

PARADOX

I know a paradox she's beautifully insane
She has many personalities
And yet she has no brain

A complex simplicity
An angel born in hell
With complimentary insults
I know her far too well

A world victorious loser
A winner of defeat
Without her contradictions
She would not be complete

She works out exactly
What she should be doing with her life
And then she does the opposite
Just like a twisted knife

And although she could achieve
So much glory if she tried
Somewhere in the corner
Is where she'll always hide.

Zombie

Undead redhead
Really hot
He should behead
But cannot

He keeps in chains
His sex slave zombie
Feeds her brains
He gains quite grimly

And when at last, policeman knocks
Undead redhead he unlocks.

SQUIRM!

Insufference of life style
Orgasm on a thread
Torture of the innocence
The infantile is dead

Corpses on a soul string
Clown upon a tree
Half a lager later
And I was never me

Welcome to the dead zone
I lust for when I can
A sequel to apocalypse
The artistry of man

Hellish is a childhood
Death is but my kind
A metaphor of over kiss
Miranda of my mind

And thus the wake of morning
I wrote this very vision
A slave to bitter innocence
The raping of dominion

Beneath the very hem line
The touching of her silence
The reconcile of incomplete
A graveyard full of violence

Until the final moment
We welcome to the crave
The sect of pure depravity
Enticement of the slave

And still the skulking mindless
We're woken to the cut
The epilogue of sinners' death
The paramount of slut

I know the world is woken
We shook her till she died
Screaming out in final pain
The words that we had lied

And now the hope is blackness
I hold you to the void
The waking of the chosen few
To feed the paranoid
Squirm!

CANDLE.

Light a candle
In the light
Cast the darkness
On your sight
This is hope
Let's make it right
Light a candle
For the night

In the darkness
In the dream
Take the life
And make it scream
In the darkness
Of mid-day
Light a candle
For the prey

As they burn
They pale away
Till candle wax
Has dripped dismay
For our cursed
May angels pray
Light a candle in the day

And if you do
Regret the deed
Cut your throat
And watch it bleed
Once a truth
We built on need
Worship death
But do not plead

Then at last
The light burns dry
No more tears
No reason why
Mine to kill
And theirs to die
When the candles
Fail to cry.

CEMETARY

In a graveyard we sit
Hold hands and play

With dolls
3am at morning
Raining heavy
We find a grave
There are many

And we dance
And we kiss
I kiss thee
Somewhere else than this

Children of the night we are
A very pretty fright we are
I hold you down
Remove your bra

And then we woke
The things asleep
And we did laugh
And they did wail
To find themselves
In slugs and snail

Hide and seek
Amongst the dead
I lose the girl

Wait
There she is
With a knife
And my life..

Is this.

I MISS U

Here I am
With friends, alone
No reception, stupid phone
Somewhere else, I'd rather be
Your embrace
The place for me

In your grip
Between your thighs
This is where
Existence lies

All is death
Except for you
And you're not here
And I am blue

Lost lethargic
All alone
No reception, stupid phone

Can not bare
To be without
The feel of you
Both in and out

Here with friends
Frolics, fun
My misery
Has just begun

And every second
Of every hour
With us apart
It breaks my heart
And all this fun
Is sour.

YOUNGER THAN LAUGHTER

Goddess
Maiden, Mother, Crone
Younger than laughter
Older than stone

Maker of mountain
Sculptor of sea
Igniter of stars
Creator of me

The beauty of nature
Reflecting your own
Goddess
Maiden, Mother, Crone

Younger than laughter
Older than stone

Powerful beyond compare
Graceful, elegant and fair
Playful, youthful
Aged and wise
Mistress of both truth and lies

Writer of the very fates
Gives potency
And castrates!

THE MOTHS COMETH

The air was thick with fairies
So thick she couldn't breathe
They pulled her down
And bound her
Held her open at the knees

The dead ones in her mouth
Muffling her pleas
The live ones in her lower down
Did mercilessly tease

She was wrought and writhing
Next day they found her dead
With moth wings all about her
Scattered neatly on the bed

Her skin had been lacerated
Her nipples had been torn
And within her rotting corpse
A million offspring born.

THE CHANGE RING

Creation of creation
The ring of total choice
The ultimate asylum
The individual voice

The object of corruption
The power true to none
The sweet seductive
'Change Ring'
Thank hell
There's only one!

NORMAL PEOPLE

Shut the fuck up
And listen to the twisted
How I adorn you
With some of my hate

This is your world
And that makes you gifted
So listen to the twisted
Now pupils dilate

Each of you listen
With no understanding
Ears have their walls
So graffiti is cheap

I'm teaching you nothing
And that is the lesson
Write me an essay
The silence of sheep!

SCREAM!

Stress the anti-constant
Is swelling to extreme
Paranoia running high
The building of the scream

It's building to a climax
The audience takes flight
The perfect note of death itself
Is playing here tonight

And then the nightmares over
The calm comes to my mind
But soon again the pressure comes
The vision for the blind

And so the earth still trembles
Waiting for the void
The coming of apocalypse
The scream of paranoid!

MORNING

Wake from the grave
To shower and shave
A toothbrush gets
Stuck in your teeth

The soap stings your eyes
You can't close your flies
And nothing
Will bring you relief!

Gosling-bumps

Things that go bump in the night
Like fat people fucking
A gruesome sight

Fingernails scratch on the door
A scream rings out
Then stops
And in the basement
The vampire hops

Are brewed to perfection
The barmaid behind the bar
Where else would she be
Moistens my erection

And all is horror
In my head
I have to blame
The books I've read
And outside
The living dead

Are waiting for their bus.

THE HALLOWEEN POISONER

Sproglins playing goblins
Witches and the damned
Knocking at my door
With their greedy little hands

Taking all I give them
With looks of pure delight
Chocolate laced with cyanide
My specialty tonight!

HAPPY X-MAS

Have you heard of Santa Claus?
He breaks in once a year
Once I made a fat git trap
But only caught reindeer!

Most would use the doorway
The window if perverse
Santa chose the chimney choice
I'll put him in a hearse!

The fire is a gas one
The gas man's never pleased
I think we'll get electric soon
Fry Santa to his knees!

Every Christmas present
He steals our food and drink
Blacks the place in chimney soot
And throws up in the sink!

A gOOd Day 4 a PiCNiC.

Little feather dancing
Floating on the breeze
The only one
That got away
From pussy in the trees!

THE GARDEN...

Living on the fringe
Of normality
In danger of going sane
Living on the fringe
Of depravity
Will someone
Please fix my brain

All I want is oddity
To let my madness grow
But weeds of utter sanity
Destroy the weird I sow!

Alice

Another thrill kill
Notched upon her bed
Busty brunette beauty
Barely bothered by her dead

Infamous psychotic
Erotic like a knife
Makes money from misery
And lives to take more life

The mage is among us
Her thoughts enough to maim
Attention needing slut bitch whore
Puts gore and bleeding into game

A roll of the dice
A dodge of dynamite
Many try to kill her
This loathsome creature of delight

She isn't joyous
She's lonely and afraid
But you might as well
Fuck in it
Once your bed is made.

EPITHANY WEIRD

Before the court
Of God she stood
A power wraith
In chain

Her eyes were pure insanity
Her mind was total pain

She focused
All her hatred
And turned
Her chains to dust

'Now Jehovah
Worship me
And grovel
Yes you must!'

Holding forth
The ring of change
She brought him
To the floor

Crucified him
Where he lay
And made him
Beg for more!

The air was filled with screaming sounds
The screaming of creation
Orgasmic as the waves of time
A throbbing death sensation

And slowly as she drained him
He spoke his final teaching
'I who know everything
Should really give up preaching!'

Vibracia

Marissa seemed quite normal
Until she turned fifteen
After that
The dizziness
Began

She would feel these odd vibrations
In domestic situations
Like from
The noises
Of her boiler
As her bubble-bath was ran

And with the most mundane of sound
It would seem to her the ground
Was spinning in the way
It really does

But she didn't seem to mind
And a straight line she could find
As she walked, in a constant state of buzz

Then before she turned sixteen
If you'll let me
Paint the scene
In a shop
In which she worked
On Saturdays

A man who held a knife
Said "money or your life"
But then she looked at him
And his whole world
Went sideways

He landed with a bump
As Marissa stood her ground
And the items from the shelves
Fell abruptly all around

And he tried to run away
But to that thief's loved ones' dismay
He was buried
Admist all items
For a pound.

In the newspaper it read
A freak earthquake made him dead
But Marissa was certain otherwise
So she dressed herself in lycra
And she called herself Vibracia
And now criminals
Do quake before her eyes!

LOST IN THE MIND OF A MANIAC
YOU'RE AN AVERAGE GUY AND YOUR NAME IS JACK.

Are you lost in my mind?
I would help you out
But I don't know the way
If I could get out of here
I wouldn't stay
Hey we're two of a kind
Both stuck in my mind

You don't belong here
But you can stay if you like
So what's your name?
Speak up
Use a mike

Come on then
I will show you around
Shall we start on the top floor
Or on the ground?

Don't touch that lever
And don't pull that chain
If you press that red button
It will mess up my brain!

Scral-wal!

A scral-wal fight
Is a fight of cats
Like a flut-flat flight
Is a flight of bats
And a bang-scrut-scrat
Is a race of rats
Yes a scral-wal fight
Is a fight of cats

For the cats come out
And they yowl all night
And they sometimes claw
And they sometimes bite

And they often hiss
And they stare for hours
And they scent the fence
And they spray the flowers

For a scral-wal fight
Leads to scral-wal wars
Of endless weeks
Of no score draws

Of dogs that bark
To support their team
Like a football match
Of the feline dream

Like Napoleon
And a certain duke
And other cats
And a mouse named Luke

They all do fight
Around the yard
Where my own old cat
Does sometimes guard

And it drives me mad
But it's great to see
When one poor cat
Has to take on three

And it takes them on
And it wins with ease
For it's a huge great beast
With ferocious fleas

And the scral-wal fights
Will never end
Till every cat
Is each's friend

Till every cat
Stands paw in paw
There'll always be
A scral-wal war!

Zidricdrake

Zidricdrake
The fire worm
The dragon of the east
Unparalleled in glory
By any mortal beast

His name is legendary
His thoughts
Make strong men weep
His taste in food is frightening
He doesn't care for sheep

He only likes the human flesh
The bones of babes he cracks
The strongholds fall
To flame and fear
When Zidricdrake attacks

The bravest men
Have fought him
The bravest men
Are dead
The little girls
Who watched them die
Forever wet the bed

Zidricdrake the monster
Tyrant of the sky
St George is dead and buried
But Zidricdrake won't die

He doesn't skulk in caverns,
In woodland or in scrub
He's hidden in the midst of things
Beneath this very pub!

Monster?

This hideous monstrosity
That shits upon the floor
It wanders round quite aimlessly
And knows not what it's for

It walks with a stagger
As if about to fall
And from its fat and shapeless chin
There drips a thread of drool

Its mouth is mostly toothless
Yet that doesn't seem to cease
The wobbling of its belly
Which daily, greatly does increase

The ugly thing
Is mostly deaf
Almost blind
Yet sees what isn't there
It wails at night, a maddening cry
Born of its own despair

And when at last
It gives us rest
And finds its own in sleep
It pukes on its pyjamas, part digested guts of sheep

O' unsightly thing
What kind of beast are thy?
It contemplates the question
Then 'Colin' comes reply.

Ghost in the post

With excited eyes
She opened her prize
Package stolen
From a neighbour's front porch

"What the fuck is this?"
Said the light fingered Miss
As what it contained
Looked like human remains
And smelled a little like pork

"It's a fucking hand
With a ransom demand
The neighbour's pretty young niece"
Afraid, the thief
Buried her find
And now the niece is deceased

Then one misty morn
Looked the thief at her lawn
And what do you think that she saw?
The ghost of a girl
Retrieving her hand
And mouthing
"I'll kill you, you whore!"

The very next night
The thief got a fright
As a hand crawled onto her knee
Whilst a few feet away
The ghost said
"You'll pay
For abandoning me."

The thief cried "I'm sorry!"
The ghost didn't care
She dragged the young woman
To the top of the stair
And I'll leave your vivid imaginations right there
Will you push
Or release, Tiffany?

NOT EVEN THE MAD!!!

A long sleeved coat
In a padded cell
Is where we're headed
To escape this hell

For you get fucked up
But there's no unfuck down
There's no known cure
To a clown with a smile
That could scare the shit
Out of a crocodile

No there's no way back
Once you've gone mad
Just drugs and lobotomies
To send you glad

And not even the mad
Would wish to be shrunk
So in our long sleeved coats
We are getting drunk

And acting sane
For it's a human right
To remain in pain

And the inhuman shrinks
Can go away
And leave the mad
Alone to play

With their dolls.

VOICE!

'When were you first crazy
Watching from your head
The ludicrous of every day
You wish they all were dead

Lying on the ceiling
You share it like a dress
The now of your tomorrow
A never ending mess

We hope you're feeling better
You hope we wet the bed
It is your medication time
And then you will be dead!'...

Sweet Tusk

Beneath the streets
The Orks still lurk
And prepare for war

But one of them
A runt named Burk
Likes to go explore

Obviously Man's world above
Is a scary place
When you're a yellow sort of green
And have tusks
Erupting from your face

So obviously being bright
(Well quite smart for an Ork)
He only leaves the caves at night
And visits carnivals

It was at his first of these he found
His most favoured food
But when he returned
Covered in candy-floss
The other Orks were rude

"Why would you want to eat that rot
When we've got
Deep fried mole
And pickled worms
And quite a lot
Of us are cannibals"

But Burk just shrugged
Because
He was
An Ork of seldom speaking
And noticed his abrasive friends
Despite themselves
Enjoyed the duck
He had procured from Peking!

Childless?

It's 3AM
She's in the bath
The light goes off
With a childlike laugh

She stands up dripping
She cannot see
The hand upon
Her naked knee

She reaches past
Turns on the light
There is no child
Within her sight

There's no-one
In the house but her
But what was that
Fast moving blur?
In the corner
Of her eye
Now she hears
A girl child cry

She runs to where
The sound occurred
But there is no-one!
She feels absurd

"I'm over tired"
She goes to bed
Then a pillow
Hits her
On the head

She jumps right out
Turns on the light
"Guess I'll get no sleep tonight"
Yet again
There's no-one there
But in the mirror
She starts to stare:

And a girl's reflection
Stands right there
Beside her
As the naked woman's
Eyes
Grow wider
The girl looks about eleven
"Has it been that long
Since the abortion?
I thought the unborn went to heaven."

"Well you were wrong
Weren't you Mother!"

ABSTRACT P O E T R Y

Something beyond myself
Silence within the thought
A nothing on life's ocean,
Nothing less than nought.
Silver in the mindmill
Behind the blades of breath
Beyond the cosmic
Plains of earth
Deceit in valid death!

Unutterable stories
Burn the fire dry
Empty screams
Of void content
The madness in my eye.

And still the tapping window
Besieged in clover green
Less a cog
And more a spring
Amidst the hate machine...

FRAGMENTS

I'm on an acid trip
From my vodka
I fail to sip
And slowly
As I start to skip
I do not know me well
This sickly sweet ferocity
This cacophony from hell
And who but I to argue
With the wet whims
Of my being
So here I'm sat with vodka
The perfectionate
Unseething
To everything I've sought
With those eyes of illness blue
And I'm talking to a shot glass
Broken by the crossed legs
I, Infatuation
Indecision, death and dust
And yet somehow I love this
This pestilence I'm being
For through these tortured
Made up eyes
Eye once more believed in
And laughter twirled away
And with it
Went
The Pumpkin smashed fragment
Of my exasperation
Driving me to subtle suicidal
Like the drummer boy drumming
In heavy sack cloth insanity
And sigh Natasha stood in stockinged feet
Ankle deep in beauty sleep
And woke to yet another void
Of endless troubled paranoid
Sheep!

WHITE SHED!

The opaque shade of white
The devil in the shed
You know the nightmare's over
When you wake up
And you're dead!

The arachnophobic spider
Will spend the glory days
In a bath tub full of hatred
Breaking mirrors in the maze.

And when the party's over
And the drink is on the ceiling
And you kissed some ugly fucker
Cause you thought they were appealing
And the madness is provoking
And you muffle up your ears
There's a spider breaking mirrors
There's a spider in your tears...

Oh, pity thy soul
Fuckwit!

A FINGER TO YOUR LIPS.

The sun lit rose shatters tear drops caressing
Thorns and petals blood red scatter depressing
Upon the cold and polished marble blue
Reflecting the dying
Of once we knew
And all it seems is dreams and screams
And unborn children
With ice-creams
How quiet it is…

42

Philosophy is a waste of thought
Just an expose
Of logic's limitation
Grown up answers being sought
With pre-teenage investigation

Round about
And round once more
Goes that thought of train
And when you think
You're at the end
You're at the start once more
To seek such answers
From ourselves
Is a mindless chore

How should we discover
That we do not know
By asking of each other
The answer surely, no.

Sister Maria Luisa

Sister Maria Luisa
Was a very fun nun
She would initiate the novices
With cunning use
Of her tongue

This charismatic twenty-something
With a beautiful face
Found favour
In her order
But brought the Church disgrace

She convinced a priest to sleep with her
By writing him a letter
That she had her friend write for her
'Cause her penmanship was better

In the letter she pretended
To be Mary mother of God
Wrote sleep with Sister Maria
For she has a lovely bod

He didn't take much convincing
Which was probably for the best
Because she often tried to poison
The ones she did detest

However
When she tried it on
With a German Princess nun
The Princess
Did confess
And Maria was undone

But despite the fact Maria
Tried to poison Princess too
The German always described the slut
As the most amazing view!

SAD FAREWELL.

There is no good
In goodbye
So I sit
And wonder why
This word of good
Was used for sorrow
Today is ours
But not tomorrow.

BROKEN DOLL

Like a broken doll
Like a broken doll
Like a broken doll
I sit
Like a broken doll
I sit
Legs out straight in front of me
Unfocused eyes unblinking
Unfocused thoughts unthinking
My cheeks awash with tears

Like a broken doll
My key is lost
I'm unwound
Will I be found
Upon the ground
I sit

Like a broken doll
Unblinking
Like a broken doll
I'm thinking
Do dolls think much at all
Do dolls think much at all
My key is lost
Or is it me
Did I have a key
Before
Like a broken doll
Like a broken doll
Am I a metaphor

Am I a metaphor
A part of me
Says simile
A doll upon the floor
Like a broken doll
I sit
Like a broken doll
I sit
Just a composite
Something must have quit
Am I really me
At all
Was I a doll before?

MY LiL PONi FUCKER

Depravity
That vile little girl
As pure as driven on snow
Hasn't got her knickers on
And makes certain that you know

Depravity
A gothy teen
Not unpleasing to the eye
But you should see
The scars she left
From toying with cacti

She's underage
And under you
And finger fucks your sister
Every other Friday night
In a game
Of incest twister

Depravity Depravity
There's no-one like Depravity
There's none with such an art
In sickening humanity

Every little fetish
Every act of immorality
Just another
Dear Diary
Written by Depravity

She eats taboos for breakfast
Then shits them on your face
Depravity
The ejaculation
In the gutter of disgrace!

WAITING

Waiting for rejection
Like mail
Repeatedly sent to the wrong address
Meant for some poor soul
Who moved away and died
Years before the pen met paper
And fell in love
With everything about her
Obsessed about her
Waiting for rejection...

It lives beneath London

It lives beneath London
And slithers and slides
In sewers and subways
It hunts and it hides

It lurks in your toilet
Just round the u-bend
Awaiting its moment
An appendage to send

Into your rectum
To look for its lunch
And pulls your spine
Through your bottom
For something to munch!

ALONE

Arrogant hate
Born from inside
Grew like a tree
Grew tall and wide
Now at its base
Shadowed and small
Sits our poor hero
Hating you all!

Petrified

"In a government funded
Secret lab
They make monsters
Mad as me"
Said a straight jacket clad
Lab technician
Perched
Upon, a pot of tea

"Let me tell you
Of the rape zombies
Lust not hunger
Is their drive
O' but the virus will still kill you
Even if you survive
The savage penetration.
I watched a drunken homeless man
Get fucked
In both his eyes!"

With that he fell
And spilt the tea
"Now listen very carefully
I must impart
With heavy heart
The truth that took
My sanity!"

Alas
I dare not now repeat
His final word
Drooled at my feet
Because once said
One's complete
...ly dead
For it turned him to
Concrete!

Discarded.

Torn and twisted
Like a poem
Discarded
Disregarded
Did not make the cut
Like a homeless junkie slut
At an interview
What could the interviewer do?
Don't call us
We'll call you
Poems scattered on the floor
Do not want them anymore
Pick them up
And put them in
To the waste paper
Basket bin
She didn't even have a phone
Waits in a call box all alone
Answers every time it rings
"O' you poor discarded things
Just like me"
Poetry
Scattered pages on the floor
All unwanted evermore.

The Uninvited (or Something Blue)

News of her wedding
The final straw
For his fragile mind
He would find her
Destroy her happiness
Like her rejection
Destroyed his dreams
Took him a while
To discover
Where and when
She'd wed another
But in finding
He began
To devise
A grisly plan
To end their day
Of utmost joy
In muffled anguished screams!

At the wedding
She was smiling
The smile he longed to see
But he wasn't there to admire
And it wasn't aimed at him

At reception
Dancing, laughter
But lurking, hidden
To follow after
He
With ambitions
Abhorrent, grim!

Just about to consummate
When he unhinged the door
His thoughts consumed with hate
He threw her
Hard
To wooden floor
Then stabbed the groom
Six times
Even
Where the moon don't shine.
Turned to her and smirking sneered
"Now at last
Your milky flesh
Your heart shaped derriere
If not your heart titanium
Be mine because I dare
To take
That part
You wouldn't give."

He grasped her and he raped her then
And there and there
While groom gurgled
Awash with blood and grief
Whilst despite anguish, pain, despair
Her attractive symphonic orgasm
More than twice
Piped
The petal scented air
The last sound that husband heard
Before became
She
A widow of
The palest white of hair

From fright and not her quite slight years
For beauty she remained
Left alive, a mess
(But as a trophy took her dress)
Exhausted, sore and drained
Yet to endure
More tears for fears realised
As slowly but surely
He found and slew
All she'd invited to that perfect view
Of her happiest smile.

Of course the cops caught up to him
And in a shoot out shot him dead
But now his ghost
Is haunting her
Each night in fright
She goes to bed

And feels the cold
Creep up her thighs
She bites her lip
And rolls her eyes
But from her throat
Through bloodied lips
Escape erotic sighs.

THE TRAIN IS LATE AND CREMATED

I have lived my life
In a fantasy
And I shall continue to dream
For there is no jubilation
In sanity
And there is perfect piece
In a scream

There is no anger animosity
No hatred, fear nor despair
There is no ugly monstrosity
For the greatest of evil is fare

And I live those daze
In a dungeon
Knowing nothing can ever get in
And I climb my way
Through suicide
And look decidedly thin

I hold a hollow example
Of that Witch never should be
And find
When awoken
The mirror is broken
And that which I'm holding
Is me

The train is late and cremated
And gutted
And slutted inside

Their stands a young girl
Who gives me a twirl
Fore running in laughter
To hide.

UMBRELLAS UP UNFURLED!

Like a flower you closed in the rain
Umbrellas up unfurled
And when it was folded again
We woke in a brighter new world

Us creatures of night in the sun
Did you knew when you did it
What you were to have done
And would you have done it again
That night when we cried in the pain

Some when stands an old empty phone box
The phone dangles now off the hook
Do you remember forever
When we stood there together
Do you remember the love in my look

I remember the hate in your eyes
I remember the hurt and the lies
The love and the laughter
The sorrow now after
After those screaming goodbyes

And so the swan sings its last song
Of all that was bitter gone wrong
No reason to care
If you're still even there
And yet I have cared for so long

How can I find peace in my rest
And how can I find better
When you were the best
Petals away in the rain
Of the flower I knew
With the eyes laughter blue
The flower who gave me such pain

For with her my heart
From the sight from the start
For with her
My heart doth remain
Like a flower you closed
But left me insane.

The House

Cold chills run up your spine
Haunting noises
A wailing whine
Mist soaked carpets
Blood dripped walls
A noose wrapped neck
Through torment falls
Several inches long ago
In the building built of woe

A child is heard but never seen
The night rings out
Blood curdling scream
Again you waken from cold sweat dream
But the nightmare lingers on

Headless horsemen ride the hall
An apparition wanders through a wall
An old lady sits in a rocking chair
But you know that she's no longer there

Something goes bump in the night
Holding on to blankets tight
Then smashingly goes out the light
And the bed begins to shake
Your night dress begins to rise
Rapidly from your thighs
And smothering your face
Muffling your pleas
As something bends you at the knees
Penetrates and leaves
You with feelings of disgrace

Running screaming from the room
You trip and fall
Down winding stairs to doom
And there you stay for evermore
Another ghost behind that door
Lurking in the gloom.

Witchcraft

Wicca me this
Wicca me that
With eye of newt
And wing of bat

Cauldron bubble
Candle ignite
Incantations in the night

In the light
Of gibbous moon
Spread the tarot
Cast the rune

Evoke the spirit
Invoke Goddess
With athame
Enchant and bless.

The Box Of Be Careful What You Wish For

The Box Of Be Careful What You Wish For
Grants the opener
Not the wish, that they make, that very moment
But the wish they've made the most
During their lives
Before the lid was lifted.

Those who insist
On growing up
Often find
That the wish
That the box
Plucks
From their mind
Is one
That they made
As a child
When their ideas
Less restrained
And their mouths
Ran wild

Some of course
Never wish at all
And to them
The box
Like life
Seems small

So what then is
Your hearts' desire
Your heart of now
And all those past
If you could
Grasp that box
To find the answer
Would you
Dare to glance?

Inside

The box is dusty.

Florence and the Machine

Big hulking thing it was
Hard to tell where the Troll stopped
And the cyberwear started
Before him stood Florence
Tiny by compare
Her hair
Damp now from effort
Clinging to her flesh

He raised his club afresh
And missed
Not for the first time
Nor for the last
He swung again
For Florence
Again she was too fast

She hit him on the counter
He barely even grunted
Maybe she'd have hurt him
If the weapon wasn't blunted

Twenty minutes later
The score was still the same
If he had just hit her once
Maybe she'd be slain

He came too close for comfort
And she smacked him once again
This time his nose, a little blood

He charged and she sidestepped
And the dance continued on
Slower now
She still a step ahead
"Stay still and you'll be dead."
I'm sure they both had thought it
But only he had sought it
And she did not oblige…

In time exhaustion called a draw.

Queen Mab's Revenge

Don't speak of Merlin
The Wizard betrayed us
Don't speak of the Christians
Who spread like a plague
Don't speak of the armies
Who came to invade us
I made Britain Pagan
And so it remains

I am, Goddess
Queen of the Fey
I am, The Morrigan
Worthy of praise
I am Mab
I bring the old ways
And I'll be, lonely
At the end of all days

Lonely because
I only remain
Angry because
My World is in pain
Rise up my children
I'm woken again
Follow me
Follow me
Through tempest I reign
Defy if you wish to be
Ruthlessly slain

Crows circle about me
Rooks cry out my name
And the Tower of London
Roosts the birds of my fame

For I never left you
I've only been sleeping
And now that I'm woken
My rage begins reaping

Some say the boy Arthur
Will return for his throne
Let him come
Let him come
With his sword
From the stone

Yet wait

That blade's broken
And so will he be
For he's a mere mortal
And I'm only ME

Excalibur rusts
In a lake with no Lady
Human polution
Has chased her away
With Arthur abandoned
Who will stand 'gainst me?
I am The Morrigan
They'll rue the day
Follow me
Follow me
Into the fray
I am The Morrigan
Don't be my prey!

The Raping Woods

Five friends went
With tents
One day
Into the woods
To drink and play

Three were girls
And two were boys
Far away
From other human noise

They built a fire
And had a snack
Then Ben went
For a wee
But did not come back

They looked for him
And they called his name
Thought he was playing
A stupid game

Then they realised
With dismay
Somehow
They had misplaced Fay

Knocked out by a hefty branch
Dragged away by roots
Fay awoke, with wrists bound
And without
Her boots

A tree was tugging
At her panties
Pulled them to her knees
Whilst brambles gripped
Her ample bosom
And began to squeeze

Jethro
Some yards away
Later
Heard her
Screams
Would he get a chance that day
To save
The woman of his dreams?

Grace and Hannah
Hadn't heard her
They just saw him
Run away

"Don't you fucking leave us!"
Grace exclaimed
But Jethro didn't stay

Jethro found Fay
In quite a state
Of undress that is
Lying in the undergrowth
With a look of bliss
"What the fuck is going on?"
He asked the pretty naked Miss

Then a tree
Hit him
In the knee
And his stumble
Ungainly
Met her luscious kiss

His look of surprise
Got even bigger eyes
When grasping tendrils
Ran up his thighs
And rapidly
Undid his flies
Then slid slowly
Up inside
The hole designed
For piss

Hannah and Grace
Heard his screams alright
But by then
Were more concerned
With what they'd learned
Of their own plight

The woodland raped them
All the night
And like a puppet master
Took delight
In making them
Caress, kiss and bite
Like an expert
Lover might
And after the final
Orgasmic height
Grace said
"I'm really sorry my sister
But you've touched me better
Than any mister."
And Hannah looked at little sis
And said "You know what
If you wish
We'll try this
Some day
Without the trees!"
Grace in reply
Mouthed softly "Please!"

So all four friends were traumatised
Even though
Some had had
Nice surprise
And a few days later
A policeman's eyes
Found Ben dead
In a compromising position
And a look on his face
That according to Grace
Who identified
Was that of a man
Who had seen an apparition
But the truth is
The way he died
Was by a large branch
That wasn't his decision!

Possessed

Lily lives almost alone
With a lesbian apparition
For when she was shopping for her home
She made the wrong decision

Whilst she was viewing
The haunted house
A whisper in her ear
Said
"It doesn't cost that much to buy
And I think you'll like it here."

Lily took the voice
As her own
For no-one else was there
And so the pretty blonde
Bought the house
That soon
Whitened
Her hair

For she would see
A brunette behind her
When glancing her own reflection
But the ghost was always gone
From sight
Under
Greater
Inspection

Young Lily
Unfortunately
Was straighter than a die
But the poltergeist
Left her
No doubts
She couldn't have a guy

For when she tried to bring a bloke
Home to poke her hole
Emma the apparition
For that was her name
Spoke loudly
"I'll take his fucking soul!"
And threw things all about
And dripped mucus
From the ceiling
And if that didn't scare him off
Quick enough
He would get this chilly feeling
As the spirit squeezed his balls!

So Lily tried to see boys
At their own abodes
But Emma was never happy
And somehow always knows
She would write SLUT in blood
Upon
All Lily's clothes

So Lily tried to sell the house
But you can foresee
Emma wouldn't let her
Screamed "You belong to me!"
She would scare away prospective buyers
Any way she could
Determined to overcome
Lily's lust of "wood"

And she would treat Lily nicely
When she was being "good"
For example lounging in the nude
Would get the laundry done
So Lily began to live
Somewhat
Like a lusted after nun

But that was not enough for Emma
Not enough at all
Lily would wake unexpectedly
With breasts awash with drool!

Mermaids & Pirates

I hear their seductive song at night
Calling me to sea
Must Mermaids delight
In, tormenting men like me?

I've known of too many souls
Drowned for their lust
Lured by tail of fish
And young woman's naked bust

Teeth as sharp as knives, lurk
Behind soft plump lips
Beauty to die for
Could sink a thousand ships

Dashed dreams upon the rocks
Directed to their doom
Not by star nor compass
But by members
Stiffening, in the gloom

Beware my son
The Siren call
So pretty on the ear
The best defence
That you possess
Is your very fear

For if it can prove stronger
Than the longing in your loins
You may well live long enough
To spend ill gotten coins

So, be a Pirate
And sail these seven seas
Just remember what I said
When you hear
The Mermaids' pleas.

Ghost of Wasp

Trapped beneath the bath
We listened to it die
We didn't cry
We didn't laugh
We just heard it
Buzz for days
First angry
Then pathetic
Then silence
That preys...
Upon the mind
If we were there
What would we find?
Dead insect that decays

And then it stung me on the lip
As it flew right through my face
For that
Wrathful wretched woeful wasp
No more could be
Contained
Within that dire and lonesome place
Where its remains remained

Beneath the bath
Where spiders laugh
At lost wasp's last grimace!

Night night

Goodnight my sweet
I like your feet
So wrap them nice and warm
And close your eyes
With lullabies
And sleep until the dawn.

YOUR TURN

Weird noise awakens
The hairs on her neck
Alone in her bedroom
The busty brunette

Listens intently
Whilst reaching her robe
The noise returns louder
Asudden
Smells like the dead
Then tentacles probe out
From under her bed

She screams and she scrambles
It grabs at her ankles
She falls on all fours
On the floor

It grips her like brambles

She cries and she writhes
Her eyes open wider
As it holds her all over
And slides something inside her

Throbbing and pulsing
Thrusting vibrating
Not just the one hole
But thrice penetrating

Her body betrays her
And starts to enjoy
Being the creature's
Latest fuck toy

Leaving her pregnant
It slides out of sight
Who will it "offer"
"Delights" to
Tonight?

The previous night's victim
A boy of nineteen
Had been less fortunate still
Failing to find a vagina
The thing
Created its own void to fill!

Queen of the Night

Hecate
Queen of the Night
Goddess of Witchcraft
Titans' delight

A share of the Earth
And the barren Sea
That's the bits
Without fish in
Were given to She

A third of the Underworld
The keys to the gates
Her puppy Cerberus
Whom all the damned hates

And up by the Stars
She has privilege too
I worship Hecate
Why wouldn't you

Hecate
Whom Zeus honoured most
Hecate
Goddess of Ghosts

She holds sway
Over so many things
She could take beggars
And raise them to Kings

The prettiest laugh
From her beautiful maw
I've met this Goddess
That I adore

Blessed by her power
Blessed by her grace
Blessed by the knowledge
Of her stunning face

Her hair is fair
Her robes are pitch
In every pack
She's alpha bitch

She is my Goddess
I am her child
Her softest whisper
Leaves thee, beguiled!

Unforgettable?

I wonder if they think of me
The faces that I used to see
It doesn't even need to be
Fondly, just remember me

Warts an' all
I know I'm horrid
Sometimes
Sweet enough
And I understand
For some of you
The smooth ain't worth the rough
But don't forget me

My histrionic heart
Cries lullabies
And hysteric laughter
Ensues
When I wake to realisation
That your thoughts
I cannot now
Bemuse.

Creepy Pasta

She was sucking on spaghetti
When it started sucking back
"What the fuck" she wondered
As she pulled it from her face
Mixing drops of youthful blood
With spaghetti from deep space

With the taste of human blood it grew
To such a massive size
That it easily over powered her
And forced apart her thighs

Then things got really saucey
Within her underwear
As it slowly slid inside her
Vagina
And her derriere

That's when her sister wandered in
And screamed in shocked surprise
But the pasta didn't mind her
Joining in
With big sister's sexual cries

So it grabbed her by the ankles and pulled the girls together
Forcing them to scissor
'Til they came in waves of pleasure!

Then they ate the pasta.

The Day The Aliens Didn't Come To Earth

It was a Wednesday in November
The day they didn't come
Instead they parked their fleet of ships
In rings around the Sun

And started to construct something
That began to block the light
It was only then
We understood
The nature of our plight

We tried to reason with them
With words
Then weaponry
But they were too advanced
To be destroyed
And just ignored our plea

So slowly then
They stole our Sun
And we were left to die
It's so cold and dark now
There's no food left
Goodbye.

Made in the USA
Monee, IL
29 December 2024

75633010R00051